Undead Ed
and the DEMON FREAKSHOW

Rotterly Ghoulstone

ILLUSTRATED BY

Nigel Baines

An Imprint of Penguin Group (USA) Inc.

Published by the Penguin Group
Penguin Young Readers Group
345 Hudson Street, New York, New York 10014, U.S.A.

USA / Canada / UK / Ireland / Australia / New Zealand / India / South Africa / China
Penguin Books Ltd, Registered Offices: 80 Strand, London WC2R 0RL, England
For more information about the Penguin Group visit penguin.com

Published simultaneously in Canada

Library of Congress Cataloging-in-Publication Data is available

ISBN 978-1-59514-533-8

Printed in the United States of America

1 3 5 7 9 10 8 6 4 2

This one is for Wendy Schofield on the occasion of her retirement from Holy Trinity School in Ramsgate.
Wendy taught some of the brightest children in England ... and me.

FIRST MISTAKE:

GETTING HIT BY A TRUCK

My name is Ed Bagley, and I'm dead. Thanks for the sympathy.

One rainy night I was hit by a truck and the lights went out. Weirdly, they came back on again and my undead "life" began. Go figure.

Being undead is like getting to a movie theater five minutes after the movie has started and then having to climb over a load of people to find your seat. Nobody really tells you anything: they expect you to find your place, keep quiet, and try to catch up on the stuff you missed.

I'm not just undead, I'm a zombie, too—that sucks more than a mansion full of vacuum cleaners. I mean, I could have been anything: a vampire, a werewolf, even a ghost. Zombies are like the tramps of the living dead: you might throw one a few kind words occasionally, but you don't want them coming over for dinner and stinking the place up.

Besides, zombies tend to leave things behind…and we're not talking hats and coats: we're talking teeth and jawbones.

Nope, we're definitely not popular…even among our kind. Fortunately, my family doesn't suffer any real embarrassment: none of the "breathers" can see us.

The worlds of the living and the dead fit together like a pair of escalators at a supermarket: one goes up, one goes down, and never the twain shall meet.

It's just as well, really: if my parents saw me right now, my mom would scream and run away, and my dad would probably call the police.

Of course, I can't help the way I am.

You know the dangerous type? Sure you do; every story has one. In *Star Wars*, it was Luke; at Hogwarts, it was Harry; in Mortlake, it's definitely me.

I'm the one who brings destruction, the one who puts everyone in danger, the one who's *letting the whole class down.*

The horrible thing, though, is that I did it all by accident.

You see, I became a zombie because—unbeknownst to me—I was cursed. There's a long version of that story and a short version. You're getting the short version, because you're probably not going to live long enough to hear the full epic: I didn't.

Basically, I got electrocuted when I was younger, and in doing so, I accidentally interrupted this weird group suicide, masterminded by an evil clown. (You should probably read over that last sentence a few times until it starts to sound slightly less warped.)

Kambo Cheapteeth was a deranged circus clown who, together with some weird friends, planned his own glorious death. Unfortunately, I messed it up for Kambo...

... and now he's equally determined to mess up my death. The hard way.

He's enlisted the help of two of his undead friends: Carble and Stein. Carble is a seriously sinister midget with a massive nose and gleaming brass teeth, while Stein has a sewn-up eye and an innate ability to float above the ground. Shudder.

If I was on my own, I'd be terrified. Unfortunately for Kambo, I've got some pretty good friends watching my back: Max Moon, a crazy werewolf with an eye for trouble, and Jemini, a highly emotional vampire who can't seem to accept the fact that she's dead.

Yeah, okay, they're not exactly the IDEAL gang, but you can't be too choosy when you

smell as bad as I do: try taping a dead mackerel to your armpits and see how many of *your* friends stick around ...

... especially if you also happen to have a feral, half-demonic hand.

That's right, there's more! During my first week in the world of the dead, I discovered that my left arm had long been possessed by Kambo's demonic soul. The trouble was, I learned this when the entire arm detached from the rest of my body and went on a mad, destructive rampage around Mortlake. I had to move mountains in order to get it back, and it hasn't been right since.

By "hasn't been right" I mean a) it now has nine fingers, four of which seem to veer away at crazy angles from the regular five, b) the fingers are *in between* the normal ones so the movement looks especially freaky to anyone who's not already insane, and c) every now and again the hand rises up and uses two of the demon fingers to flick the end of my nose, for reasons I haven't yet worked out. This last development is particularly worrying, as the end of my nose has already dropped off twice.

Still . . . you've got to laugh, right?

SECOND MISTAKE:

UPSETTING THE DEAD

People think it's not possible for the dead to die ... and they're wrong. It's called Eviction: in plain speech, it means "death for the dead." Only evil spirits tend to be able to cause it, because no one else in their right mind would ever try. Largely, the dead respect one another, and believe it or not, there's a great sense of community among the undead.

Tonight was a great example of that.

According to Evil Clive, it was the biggest gathering of the dead in Mortlake for over a hundred years. I stood on a raised platform in the old town hall, feeling like a prize idiot, as the eyes of vampires, werewolves, ghosts, ghouls, spirits, and various other deadies goggled at me with a mixture of fascination and hatred.

The meeting was about to start, but I simply couldn't take my mind off the main attraction. (Well, I guess if you were standing in the crowd, the main attraction was me—after all, the single reason for everyone gathering here was my arrival in Mortlake.) However, for me, the one thing that grabbed my attention and simply wouldn't let go was the hideous sight of Ten Toe Tom: I had, in all honesty, never seen anything like him in my life or my death.

Ten Toe Tom wasn't just dead. He was an eater of the undead . . .

. . . and he was massive.

MASSIVE.

10

MASSIVE.

That man, I thought, *is bigger than an elephant.*

No, I corrected myself, *he's bigger than ten elephants.*

Rubbish, said an inner voice, *he's bigger than an elephant ARMY.*

Tom quite literally spilled out in every direction, sprawling all over the inside of the hall. I still didn't fully understand the overlapping barrier between the worlds of the living and the dead, so I didn't have a CLUE how they'd even moved him inside: the double doors at the front of the hall weren't big enough to admit one of his chins.

"I didn't expect to see *him* here," Max whispered, nodding at the mass of flesh with a look of mild surprise. "I can't remember the last time any of us actually saw Tom. . . ."

"The night Evil Clive fought the ghouls outside the old graveyard," said Jemini, sweetly. She was standing on my other side, patting me companionably on the arm. "Don't worry, Ed. Everything will be okay. Don't feel bad or anything. It's only a meeting to let everyone know that Cheapteeth might attack us all because of you."

I smiled weakly and looked back at the blob in the crowd.

"Why is he called Ten Toe Tom?" I asked. "Surely there're other ways to describe him? I mean, we've *all* got ten toes; I don't see why—"

"It's Ten TOW Tom, you doofus," Max muttered, covering his mouth and snickering. "On account of the fact that it takes ten tow trucks to move him anywhere."

"Oh . . . right. I see. But—but how did he get like *that*?"

"He's an eater," Jemini said, matter of factly.

"Like the ghouls?"

She shook her head. "No, the ghouls just chew on corpses. Tom actually eats undead beings—but he doesn't process them, so they're just down there, in his stomach, waiting . . ."

"Waiting?" I gasped. "Waiting for what?"

"Maybe some toilet time," said Max, snickering again.

I just stared at him.

"Seriously, dude . . . if he EATS the dead, how come this room hasn't cleared out? I mean, it's like living people standing next to a tiger or something. . . ."

Max grinned, but it was Jemini who spoke.

"Eaters like Tom only have a taste for wicked souls . . . so, as long as you're not actually EVIL, you'll be okay."

I looked down at my hand and gulped, but

15

I didn't have time to ask them anything else because at that moment Evil Clive got to his feet and the entire hall sputtered into silence. Evil Clive was an animated human skeleton who, for reasons still unclear to me, governed the dead in Mortlake. He wore a dirty gray raincoat and a baseball cap.

"Dead of Mortlake!" he cried out. "Hear me now! Hear me, or I'll curse you all to the fires of infinity!"

Clive looked down at the audience, but there wasn't much of a reaction. If anything, they looked *bored*.

I guess that was the problem with being dead; it was difficult to take any sort of threat seriously.

"As many of you will have heard," Clive continued, "a cursed child has come among us: one who requires our help and protection in these dark days ahead...."

"Why should we help him?" shouted a vampire at the front of the crowd. "We don't even *know* him!"

"Yeah!" echoed a werewolf on the other side of the room. "We didn't ask him to rise up in our town, the zombie freak!"

A chorus of jeers exploded in the hall. I tried to act as if the whole scene wasn't bothering me, but a can of lemonade flew out of the crowd and knocked my jaw off, and I spent the next few seconds scrambling around on the floor, trying to find it.

"He stinks!" came a cry from the front row, who were all leaning back and covering their noses.

"Nothin' stinks more than your attitude, bloodsucker!" Max yelled, pointing at the vampire who'd made the remark and trying to ignore Jemini, who resented the term and was glaring at him.

As if to underline her anger, she suddenly stepped forward, stood in front of both Max and me, and clapped her hands loudly until all the jeering died down.

"Ed is my friend," she said. The statement took me a bit by surprise, as I'd always felt that Jemini only *tolerated* me . . . at best. "None of us wanted to die—the shadow fell upon all of us. But at least, in death, many of you can live peacefully. Well, Ed doesn't have that opportunity. He's being stalked—even in his

death—by the same evil that plagued him in life. Give him a chance. PLEASE."

I tried to block out some of Jemini's words, mainly to stop myself from tearing up, but the continuing jeers from the crowd quickly helped me replace my appreciation of her support with grim anger.

"Who cares?" shouted a vampire from the back row.

"Yeah," echoed another werewolf.

"QUIET!" screamed Evil Clive, jumping up and down like an enraged puppet. "Don't test me, you worthless graveworms! One more bleat from any of you and Tom will be EATING the culprit. Need I say more?"

Finally, *now* there was silence. It seemed that no one fancied being Tom's afternoon snack.

"Right," Clive said, adjusting his baseball cap so that the brim was facing backward.

"First, we're protecting this boy because he's one of *ours*. He died within the city limits and he's underage. Therefore, he's our responsibility. Second, we're not just protecting Ed, we're protecting ourselves. The more observant of you will have noticed that a ghostly circus has taken up residence in Midden Field. Now, we don't know what dark, arcane magic is being used to power it *or* to generate its weird and wild inhabitants . . . but we DO know that the entity behind it wants our young friend destroyed. I want every undead citizen of Mortlake on the lookout for—"

Evil Clive suddenly glanced over at me and raised his hands. "Come on, boy—this is your fight, isn't it? Tell us exactly who we're up against."

I felt every watery, glaring (and in one case oozing) eye in the room fixed on me.

"Er . . . Kambo Cheapteeth," I managed,

smiling weakly and trying to ignore the fact that my bad hand had begun to twitch and spasm like a fish in a catcher's net. "He's an—er—an undead circus clown. He's got—um—a rotting face, runny makeup, and . . . er . . . big shoes."

This little speech hadn't exactly ignited the room, but I plowed on anyway.

"Then there's Vincent Carble. He's a really sinister little midget who sometimes crawls along on all fours. He's got a massive nose and brass teeth."

Looking out at the crowd, I definitely saw one or two expressions that suggested I was making the whole thing up.

"And, er, finally there's Jessica Stein. She's kinda like one of those voodoo dolls or that girl from the horror movies with all the hair over her face. She's got a sewn-up eye—oh, yeah, and she can float in the air."

This time, rather oddly, all the murmurs were positive. Apparently, the undead community of Mortlake couldn't believe in mutant clowns or a big-nosed midget, but they were definitely down with floating, one-eyed voodoo girls. The room was now buzzing. Admittedly, the vampires still didn't look happy, but most of the others at least seemed *reluctantly* ready to help.

I looked down at my hands and realized I was shaking.

The battle had begun.

THIRD MISTAKE:

OPENING MY BIG FAT MOUTH

It was a gray afternoon, and the threat of storms was clear in the sky over Mortlake.

Jemini was skipping.

Skipping.

"She's very special, isn't she?" I said to Max, as we climbed the long, high hill that overlooked the town.

Before the werewolf could answer, Jemini stopped in her tracks and spun around.

"I can *hear*, you know. I'm a vampire—I'm not deaf. Besides, what's wrong with skipping, Ed? Huh? Don't you ever feel happy for no good reason? Don't you ever feel like—I don't know—just reaching out and giving the world a great big hug?"

Max and I shared a glance.

"Not recently," I admitted. "But sometimes I do feel like giving it a darn good k—"

"C'mon," Max interrupted. "Time's racing on. We need to keep moving."

Jemini skipped off once again, propelling herself up Prospect Hill with the kind of enthusiasm you'd usually find in a toddler. However, she hadn't gone more than a few yards when she suddenly stopped. Her head dipped, her shoulders hunched up, and she began to shake.

Now she's crying, I thought. *What gives?*

I wanted to go and ask her about it, or at least offer her a few words of comfort, but Max seemed to detect my intentions and held me back.

"Don't," he muttered. "Believe me, there's nothing in the world you can do to make Jemini feel any better about the stuff she's going through. Don't let any of it change your opinion of her, though: I tell you, buddy—she's a really good person."

I looked at Max and tried to read his expression. "What is wrong with her?" I asked, searching his face for an answer. "It's something to do with how she died, right? She drowned?"

Max sighed and looked down at his feet for a long time before he replied.

"You know how you hate being a zombie, Ed?"

"Yeah. Totally."

"Right. Well—and you can trust me on this—you'd really, *really* hate being Jemini."

Max hurried up to the vampire girl and gently moved her along the path. We walked in silence from that point, until Jemini suddenly cleared her throat and pointed ahead of us to the crest of the hill.

"Ed, we're here! This is the safe house Evil Clive wants you to use! It's going to be fun—like one big sleepover!"

I looked from the safe house to Max and back again. My jaw dropped, but at least it didn't fall off. . . .

"You can't be serious." I gawked up at the wrecked outline of the massive building perched on the crest of the hill. "How can you call this a 'safe' house? It doesn't even look safe to be *in*. For starters, half of it's missing!"

Max gave me a lopsided, guilty grin, but Jemini cut him off before he could offer any sort of explanation.

"It was Evil Clive's idea," she stated, shoving past the pair of us and making her way directly up the hill. "It's the highest point overlooking Mortlake. It will be easier for Cheapteeth's demons to find you here."

Easier to find me? I played these words over and over in my head, but they sounded *wrong*.

"I thought the idea of a safe house was that the bad guys *wouldn't* find you," I complained, reluctantly following the receding vampire girl.

"Evil Clive reckons we should dangle you like bait in front of Cheapteeth," Max muttered, keeping pace with me. "You know, so that he sends his minions to try to snatch you."

"And that's what he *wants* to happen?"

"Yeah, I guess."

I looked up at the wreckage once again. It loomed large against the murky skyline. Seemingly half the house was missing: I could see open rafters and gaping holes in lower outlying roof sections, and the east wall was no more than a stack of crumbling bricks around an old stove.

I remembered the place from my school days. They called it Prospect Hall, which always made me laugh. The locals avoided it, partly because it was rumored to be haunted, but mostly because it was structurally unstable and had claimed the lives of at least three builders.

In the normal world, no one lived there and the entire building had long been abandoned. However, the dead had definitely been busy here. . . .

"Get ready to meet someone very special," Jemini said cheerfully.

To my astonishment, she marched up to the house and knocked on the front door. This was particularly pointless as we could all see an old lady sitting beside the fireplace *through* the front-room wall and could have easily just shouted to her instead. It took nearly ten minutes for the door to open, and—when it did—the frame shifted several inches.

There, outlined in the doorway, was the ugliest woman I've ever seen in my life.

There were spots on top of moles on top of boils: the massive wart on the side of her neck had so much hair that for a second I actually thought there was someone else standing *beside* her.

"Hello, Jem," she said, with more of a grimace than a smile. "You all had better come inside; I was told to give you some dinner."

Jemini nodded, stepped into the door-way, and turned around to beckon us forward.

"You already know Max," she muttered. "The other one is Ed Bagley. Ed, this is Mrs. Looker."

I wasn't prepared for the name: I just wasn't. I tried really, really hard to keep a straight face...but I still spat out my tongue, and part of my cheek landed on Mrs. Looker's left shoe.

I was apologizing on and off for the next hour, even as the poor old crone was dishing up milk and cookies. To make matters worse, half the flesh around my stomach flopped onto what remained of the carpet, so the first cookie I ate landed in a series of mushy puddles around my feet.

"So . . . er . . . thanks for letting me stay here, Mrs. . . . Looker," I said, trying to divert attention from the mess on the floor.

The old woman nodded, and I noticed that her eyes were glowing blue. "That's okay, dear. I don't get many visitors these days . . . and, of course, I can't leave."

"Mrs. Looker is a gaunt," said Jemini instructively. "Gaunts are like ghosts, except they're not allowed to wander. Mrs. Looker is cursed to haunt this house for all eternity."

"Wow," I said. "That really sucks—this place is a serious dump. You must—"

Max elbowed me in the ribs.

"This was my family home, dear," Mrs. Looker said, without even the slightest trace of anger or upset. "I'm afraid it's gone to ruin over the last few years."

I was about to mutter some feeble attempt

at an apology when Jemini leaned over and whispered in my ear.

"Her husband is still alive. He's in a nursing home in the living world—it's best just to let it be."

I smiled weakly at the gaunt but couldn't help feeling a bit sad for her. There were ghostly photographs of the old woman's family *everywhere*.

"You're not looking too good, pal."

The statement had come from Max, and looking down at myself, I could see he was right.

My flesh, which had until now been dropping off in ugly lumps and leaving me looking like a giant walking slab of Swiss cheese, was beginning to change. A horrible, sallow shade had seeped beneath it, and every layer looked stretched in some way, like plastic wrap gets if you pull it tight over the top of a jar.

I was, quite literally, rotting away.

The others were staring at me, all except Mrs. Looker, who was holding down the tablecloth so that it didn't blow away in the wind.

I didn't want to ask the question, but I couldn't help myself—I had to know. "What happens when this all peels off? Do I just . . . disappear?"

Jemini, the world's foremost source of knowledge on everything, shook her head. "No, you shed back to the bone."

For a moment, I just gawked at her. Then I put two and two together, and my eyes widened.

"Is Evil Clive a *zombie*?" I sputtered, starting to rise from my chair. "Is that why he's so determined to protect me, because I'm like him?"

A deathly silence settled over the table, but it was interrupted when part of the living room wall suddenly imploded, spewing several bricks onto the threadbare carpet.

Max immediately assumed a sort of half-wolf shape: it was a warning sign I'd seen a few times before, like a dog sensing danger.

I got to my feet as quickly as I could.

Two werewolves forced their way through the gap in the wall, then parted to admit the sad and bedraggled form of Forgoth the Cursed. I'd only met little Forgoth once, but while the kid was undoubtedly pathetic to look at, he was certainly worth having around in a fight . . . as was Mumps, the free-roaming demonic entity who masqueraded as his teddy bear.

Max immediately sprang to his feet, one

eye on the cloud-covered moon. Even Jemini and Mrs. Looker became visibly tense.

"What—" I started, but Forgoth put a finger to his lips and pointed up at the sky.

"They're coming," he whispered. "And there are *loads* of them."

FOURTH MISTAKE:

NOT RUNNING AWAY ~~AWAY~~

Forgoth was puffing and panting, green mist and ghostly essence spilling out around him like a cloud of dust. I couldn't guess exactly how a phantom might run out of breath, but he was certainly showing all the signs of heavy exhaustion.

"C-C-Clive asked me to keep a watch on Cheapteeth's circus," he managed, as we all gathered around him. "B-but as soon as I arrived on the edge of the field, all these flaps opened up in the big top and a load of demons flew out."

"Demons?" Max asked, sharing a pained glance with Jemini.

Forgoth nodded. "Small, red, and spindly with sharp teeth and leathery wings. They look like a red cloud when they're all together. The midget and that weird floating girl with the sewn-up eye left with them. They're heading this way."

"We should run!"

The words were Max's, not mine, but my formerly possessed left hand twitched at the merest suggestion of fleeing from Kambo Cheapteeth.

Did I mention how much I hate being a zombie? Oh good, thought I might have forgotten to do that.

"So . . . do we run or not?" Max repeated.

As usual, he and Forgoth were looking at Jemini and everyone was ignoring *my* opinion completely, despite the fact that if the demons *did* turn up, it would be me they'd carry off in a cloud of zombie dust. I was getting increasingly annoyed at just being ignored; everyone seemed to know more about my situation than I did, and no one ever managed to spare the time to fill me in. It was like constantly being at a surprise birthday party you hadn't wanted.

"Evil Clive sent you here for a reason," Mrs. Looker announced. It *sounded* like there would be more to her announcement, but she didn't actually say anything else.

Yet another mysterious message with no apparent meaning.

I felt my hand twitch suddenly, and every muscle in my body tensed.

Suddenly there was an ear-splitting thunderclap and a streak of lightning that seemed to come straight out of a B horror movie and into my face.

Literally.

"Argh!" I screamed, jumping about three feet in the air.

"Ed!" Jemini shouted, rushing over but stopping short of actually touching me. "Are you okay? You just got electrocuted!"

"Really?" I yelled back, my fingers finding a lump of charred flesh where the crest of my skull used to be. "Do you think?"

"Bad luck, dude," Max growled. "That's mental. Seriously, of all the places it could have hit!"

"Yeah," I muttered, picking at bits of my head and flicking them spitefully at the walls. "I thought the same when the truck got me."

The second flash of lightning seemed to go on forever and lit up the afternoon sky around Prospect Hill.

I really wish it hadn't.

FIFTH MISTAKE:

TRYING TO TAKE ON AN ARMY

To say the demons occupied the sky in every direction would have been an understatement: they *were* the sky.

It took me a while to realize that each tiny gap between two demons was in fact filled ... by at least two other demons. They were horrible, spindly, chittering humanoids with long claws, screwed up faces, and leathery wings.

The sky was *heaving* with them.

"We're mincemeat," Max whispered, eyeing the writhing mass of bloodred skins. "Well, I mean, you are already, but—"

"Look!"

Everyone stopped talking when Jemini pointed a shaking finger at the middle of the floating army. There, supported on a cushion of her own bizarre airstream, was Jessica Stein, Kambo Cheapteeth's demented sidekick.

I couldn't get the word *harpy* out of my head whenever I looked at her.

She hovered on the wind like some giant insect, hair plastered over her sallow face and black, rotting teeth forcing her mouth into a sick smile. Her one good eye was hidden under the flow of jet locks, while its opposite continued to ooze freely from the stitches that held it firmly shut.

Thanks to Jemini's brilliant research skills, we now knew a lot more about Miss Stein than we had when I first ran into her. A tightrope walker with a love of unspeakable heights, she'd been committed to a lunatic asylum after she went wild during a show and started to randomly attack the audience. Before the police could capture her, however, she'd broken into a shop that sold doll's houses and sewn one of her own eyelids shut. No one knew why.

What we did know was that in death she could float unaided and had claws like a dragon.

"Run!" Forgoth shouted, shaking me from my reverie. *"Run!"*

"NO! STAND YOUR GROUND! THEY *WILL* NOT ENTER THIS HOUSE!" Mrs. Looker cried, throwing out her hands in a wild gesture. All the doors and windows slammed shut, some with such force that a line of terrible cracks appeared in the plaster. The house on Prospect Hill had sealed like Fort Knox in a matter of seconds.

I would have been quite impressed had it not been for the fact that we were watching the sky through a hole in the living room wall.

We didn't get much time to dwell on this, as it was at that precise moment that the demons fell on us like a rogue wave in a surfing competition, breaking over the house in their hundreds.

"They can't enter the house," Jemini whispered excitedly, as several of the gangly creatures dived for the gap in the wall only to recoil as if they'd flown into a hot griddle. "It's Mrs. Looker—she's done something to the boundaries."

The two werewolves who'd accompanied Forgoth through the wall immediately took

to
their
heels, furring
up and howling
like the wind as they
exploded from the house
and tore into the demons.

Half submerged in the throes
of change, both werewolves hit the
demon swarm with a bang. Two of the hideous

creatures immediately flew back into the air, somersaulting over each other and screaming in frustrated anger at the strength of the frenzied attack. But victory for the werewolves was short lived: two demons cast aside became four swooping back; three ripped apart became six fresh and ready to bite.

"They're two of my pack," Max growled, his teeth and fingernails beginning to lengthen. "And they're not at their strongest without moonlight. I can't just stand here with you guys and watch them shredded in front of me."

"Maximus Moon," Jemini said, turning to glare at him. "Don't you DARE go out there."

But she was talking to dead air: the wolf leapt through the hole and tore to the defense of his friends, just as another batch of demons lunged out of the sky.

"Max!" Jemini screamed, leaning out of the

opening in the brickwork and making frantic gestures with her arms. "Max!"

Blue coils of electricity covered the holes in the house like fishing nets, repelling the demons at every point. Mrs. Looker muttered under her breath, snakes of energy crackling from her hands and feet as her eyes rolled back inside her head. As a further raft of electric tendrils danced from her shoulders and sizzled all over the house, she snatched hold of Forgoth, preventing the little phantom from leaving the house.

More and more demons flocked to attack Max Moon, and I watched with mounting horror as he reared and struck out in full were-wolf form, sending several of the fiends somersaulting backward amid spiraling sprays of their own glistening green blood.

Well done, Ed. A voice cackled inside my head, and it had an edge to it. I couldn't tell if it was my own voice or the voice of Kambo that dwelled in my hand . . . or even some strange mixture of the two, but it was definitely talking to me.

That's the spirit. Watch your friends suffer and die while you're safe on the inside, protected, coddled, safeguarded by the old witch woman. There's a word for what you are, Ed—a word that sums up exactly what you're all about.

COWARD.

Max was losing the fight. Max Moon, my first real friend in the world of the dead, was being forced to his knees by the demon horde, while their cackling and demented ghoul of a leader hovered in the sky and clapped her hands with unconcealed glee.

COWARD.

Mrs. Looker threw me a warning glance, but she'd have needed an army to stop me from hitting the hillside.

I might be a pathetic, putrid, stinking zombie, and I might be losing more and more flesh by the day . . . but I was still possessed of a limb that had single-handedly eviscerated packs of ghouls and an entire clan of revenants. It was time to fight.

I exploded from the opening in the wall and half rolled, half fell down the hillside. It wasn't the way I'd planned to enter the fight, but my right leg crumbled a bit so I went down pretty much on impact.

The demons were on me before I'd even had a chance to roll over. Flapping their leathery wings, they wrenched me up and into the air.

They were deceptively strong and about twice as savage as they'd seemed when viewed from the house: I was in big trouble.

A rain of tiny-clawed hands carved into me, ripping slits in my face, arms and stomach, while two different sets of needle-teeth fastened on my thighs and ankles. I was being eaten alive.

I screamed with rage and frustration, turning and twisting to escape the millions of tiny points that seared into my flesh like burning needles, forcing every nerve in my body to throb with sudden, terrible agony.

The pain was unbearable, even for a dead guy like me.

Max Moon was faring slightly better, maybe due to my arrival, and had fashioned a rhythm of ferocious lunacy that seemed to be holding the flock at bay. He looked like a ball of hair, teeth, and claws being spun on some sort of wild axis. At least he was holding his own.

I wriggled with all my might, gasping a few torn breaths and watching through tear-streaked eyes as more and more of the little crazies cannoned into me, fastening themselves onto my rotting corpse with every means at their disposal.

This was a slaughter.

To make matters worse, I was being lifted further and further from the ground. Raised into the air and held aloft like some teddy bear snatched by a claw in a mechanical toy dispenser, I caught a sudden surge of fear as the demons began to fly *apart*. The pain still throbbing through multiple bite and claw wounds, I craned my neck around to see what was happening.

At first, I suspected they might be trying to quarter me. There were at least three on each of my limbs, and their wings were beating furiously.

Then, just when I thought things couldn't get any worse, they suddenly did.

The demons weren't trying to quarter me, after all.

They were holding me out like a prize...

...a prize for *her*.

Jessica Stein, glaring down at me from lofty heights with her one good eye, let out one last crazy, blazing cackle...and dived.

I closed my eyes out of sheer terror but couldn't keep them shut. Evidently, some twisted part of my own frantic mind wanted me to *see* exactly what was going to happen to me at the hands of this demented nether-witch. I tried to scream as the evil monster soared through the air with her skirts flapping and lank hair spraying out in all direct-ions. Then something unexpected happened, not to me but to Stein herself.

She collided with Jemini in midair, and the pair slammed together so hard that they actually turned over several times and seemed to spin away toward the trees. There was a brief cheer of support from Max and the werewolves, and then the fighting intensified.

Disappointed that their mistress was now preoccupied, the demons set to work on shredding me once again, this time dragging me even further into the frosty sky.

I screamed as a new wave of pain hit my arms and legs, and it was then I realized that the pain wasn't evenly balanced.

My arm—*the* arm—hadn't been touched. I glanced along the limb, still writhing in pain, only to see that three demons were supporting it with tremendous care, while the other arm was practically being sawn off.

They don't want to upset it, I thought, trying to work things out through each fresh new bite of agony. *They don't want to ... disturb it.*

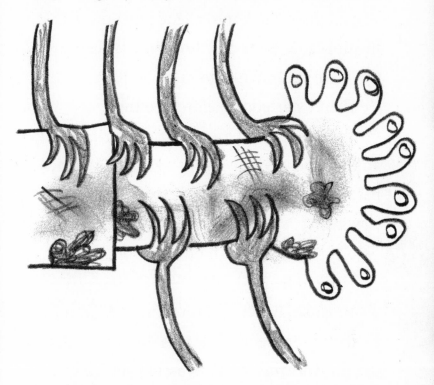

"Wake up, darn you!" I screamed, trying to flail the limb around so that I could use it. "Why won't you do anything for me, you stupid, useless, cursed-up arm!"

Nothing.

Then a thought struck me.

I twisted around in the air, using all my strength to crouch into a fetal position so that the dozen demons crawling over my extremities were all drawn together.

Then I started thrashing around.

The unexpected move caused a grim panic among the demons, who—as I had anticipated—went into a mad frenzy of biting and clawing...

...and one of them bit my hand.

The *bad* hand.

To this day, I still don't know what happened. One second I was being held in the air and the next I was falling. All I do know was the hand immediately reared up and crushed several demonic heads into a squishy pulp as if it was squashing a bug between two fingers. Others were slashed open, ripped apart, or thrown away like boomerangs . . . and this all happened in midair.

I hit the ground with an almighty thud and winced as my bad hand flipped me away from the ground and propelled me onto my feet.

Before I could even cough or cry out, the hand snatched two more demons from the air and slammed them together like a pair of coconuts.

Now I saw something emerging through the sea of red mist.

The cavalry was arriving. I felt a surge of relief flood through my exhausted body, but my hands and legs wouldn't stop shaking. Moving my limbs was fast becoming a skill: I was like some mad puppet master controlling a dummy with only half the strings.

I shook my head and peered at the mist once again.

Help was at hand.

A truck cab, one of the largest I'd ever seen on the front of an eighteen-wheeler, slammed through the wall of flapping demons and rolled on up the hill, emitting a loud blast from its horn as it screeched to a halt.

Evil Clive sprang from the driver's seat and hit a button on the side of the truck. The trailer began to unfold like a flower and revealed the immense bulk of Ten Tow Tom.

A loud and fearful chittering rang through the cloud of demons, and the front line broke rank and began to disperse. Their desire to snatch and shred me was slightly outweighed by a determination *not* to get devoured.

Evil Clive's arrival also triggered Forgoth's escape from the protective clutches of Mrs. Looker. The little phantom erupted from the front door of the house and threw Mumps onto the ground, birthing a wave of low ground rumbles as the free-roaming demonic entity took form. Great furry arms and legs sprouted from either side of the teddy bear as its massive and shaggy body caught up with the rest of its mutated growth. The head seemed to inflate like a giant balloon, sprouting random tufts of stuffing and a set of teeth that made it look more like an ogre than a child's toy. Roaring loudly, it tore toward the quivering army of red.

To my surprise, the demons didn't retreat. They simply flew to a greater distance, regrouped, and came back in a fresh new wave.

The sea of gleaming critters swarmed and massed like a million tiny insects converging on a cow pie, their leathery little wings flapping madly in the breeze.

They broke over the giant, hairy body of Mumps, catching in the creature's tangled fur and biting, clawing, and scratching with

all their might as it began to peel them off in twos and threes, hurling the little critters in every direction. A few landed within reach of Ten Tow Tom, who simply snatched them out of the air and ate them, chomping happily on demon skulls as if he was enjoying a night out at a really high-class restaurant.

Evil Clive was evidently adept at killing demons and had adopted the very curious method of using his own femur bone as a baseball bat. It was working surprisingly well, and he was definitely scoring: a few even disappeared over the roof of the house.

The battle ended, quite simply, with a scream of rage.

Jessica Stein reappeared over the edge of Mortlake Wood and flew toward Prospect Hill like some sort of twisted superhero, a trail of dark energy seeping out behind her.

As the horrible, drawn features and sewn-up eye loomed into view, the freakish hag continued on her flight and vanished into the distance. The sea of demons quickly broke off the battle and followed her, just as the sun broke through the clouds and bathed the hilltop in late afternoon light.

The demons were gone, and it was just as well: despite the appearance of Evil Clive and Mortlake's admittedly terrifying eater, I didn't actually think we were winning.

As it turned out . . . I was right.

SIXTH MISTAKE:

GETTING A FRIEND INTO TROUBLE

I collapsed. I actually collapsed.

I've seen people do it in movies—fold up as if all the energy had drained out of them—but I've never hit the ground as hard as I hit it after the demon fight on Prospect Hill. I practically bounced.

Max was at my side in seconds.

"Ed, you okay? You look terrible."

I *felt* terrible, but somehow I managed a weak thumbs-up. In the background, I was vaguely aware of a cleanup operation in progress, though Evil Clive had taken Ten Tow

Tom back to whatever dark pit passed as his daily dwelling place.

Again, Max's voice shook me from my semi-conscious state.

"Can you move, buddy?"

I shook my head. "I don't know if I *can*, but I know I don't want to. Max—you're my Dead Buddy, right?"

"Of course."

"So tell me—is it true?"

The werewolf looked at me with a blank expression. "Huh? Is what true?"

"*Is* Evil Clive a zombie? Am I going to end up just like him?"

To my surprise, Max grinned.

"You've just been in a sky fight with an army of demons and a screaming voodoo girl, and the only thing you're worried about is whether or not you're going to lose more weight? Unbelievable."

I tried to smile but couldn't quite manage it. The thought of becoming a skeleton was more terrifying to me than any fight: Clive seemed so . . . well, *empty*.

When I looked up again, Max had a strange, faraway look in his eyes. He was glancing around the hillside, a slight panic surfacing in his voice.

"Where's Jemini?" he said. "Anyone seen her?"

There was no reply from the others; everyone else was either tending to their wounds or, in the case of the werewolves, trying to return to human form. Max always changed very quickly. I guess it was because he pretty much looked like a werewolf even in his human form.

"Jemini?" he asked again. "Did anyone see where she went?"

I glanced around the hillside, a sick feeling growing in my stomach. I forced myself up from the ground and began to scan the area. The truth was, I hadn't seen Jemini since she'd collided with Stein and they'd both whizzed off toward the forest.

I pointed vaguely in what I thought was the right direction.

"She tried to take on that demented Jessica Stein when she came for me," I explained, feeling really guilty. "They flew over those trees."

Max didn't hesitate, he simply took off. I followed him as closely as I could manage.

Mortlake was surrounded on three sides by forest, which became a thick wood on the downward slopes that ran to the sea.

By the time I puffed and panted my way to the first line of trees, Max had already dropped onto all fours and was enthusiastically sniffing the ground. If he'd still been in wolf form,

sorry, old habits die hard!

this would have looked perfectly normal. As it was, he reminded me a bit of a crazy uncle my family had had committed just before we moved to Mortlake. I never did find out what was wrong with the guy.

"Picking anything up?" I ventured, limping over to stand beside him. "I can't see how you would. They *flew* out here."

"I'm not tracking for scent," Max explained, getting to his feet and pointing at a sight that literally made my stomach turn. "I'm tracking blood."

I guessed it could have been worse, but the single splash of red liquid filled me with unspeakable dread. Of all the people I'd met in the underworld of Mortlake, Jemini was probably the one I found most difficult to get along with: she was miserable, bossy, and overemotional, and she dwelled on her own death to the point of insanity. But I *did* like her, and the thought of anything horrible happening to her simply because she'd tried to protect me was just … well, *horrible*.

"It might not be *her* blood," I hazarded, as Max and I both began to move into the wood. "I mean, she is a vampire, and she's pretty tough."

"She's no demon," Max growled, and for the first time I could see how worried he was. "Besides, I saw Stein fly away with the rest of her army."

We proceeded, stopping several times when Max smelled further drops of blood. It was a strange and terrible trail, one neither of us really wanted to get to the end of.

Unfortunately, we *did*.

We found Jemini lying in a clearing, her body bathed in sunlight.

She looked bad.

"Should we get her out of the light?" I asked, feeling stupid when Max simply shook his head and crouched down beside her.

"Vampires don't burn in direct sunlight," he growled. "It's a myth, like werewolves needing the moon to transform. Breathers love making stuff up."

Jemini was shaking. Tears streamed from her eyes, her clothes were ripped in places, and blue veins stood out on her neck and face. A strange, mottled pattern was visible beneath her skin, and a line of purplish liquid ran from her neck onto the forest floor.

"What happened?" Max said, putting one hand under the vampire girl's neck and lifting her head slightly.

"Shbtme," came the croaked, garbled reply. I winced as I noticed some blood caked around her teeth. "Sbtmee, Shebitme."

Max turned Jemini's head, and we saw that the horrible plethora of colors on her flesh all stemmed from a vicious wound in her neck. To say it looked infected was an understatement: it was literally bulging with poison.

"What do we do?" I asked, helping Max

lift her off the ground. "She looks like she's dying!"

"We need to get her to Clive," Max snapped.

"Can he heal her?"

The werewolf shook his head. "No, but he might be able to tell us what sort of venom she's been hit with: I'm guessing Stein isn't your everyday sort of demonic witch."

Jemini lost consciousness as we carried her back out of the wood and up the lower slopes of Prospect Hill. It was just as well: she'd obviously been in a world of agony.

"Max," I said, as I noticed my right arm beginning to rip away from my shoulder socket. "I think you better support her by yourself—I'm coming apart at the seams, here."

The werewolf nodded and took the full weight of Jemini, holding her with extreme care, and we climbed the hill.

I felt my eyes begin to fill with tears and quickly wiped them with one stinking, half-rotted hand.

"I'm sorry, friend," I muttered, my lips trembling. "This is all my fault."

Max merely shrugged, and his mouth tightened in a grim smile.

"We've all got enemies, Ed," he muttered. "It just so happens that yours are worse than most."

I smiled, but the anger inside me was practically boiling over. It really was all my fault, and now a poor vampire girl with a mountain of her own problems was going to experience a world of grim agony just for trying to help me . . . just for being my friend. How was that fair? Well, if Cheapteeth's plan was to isolate me from my friends by killing them all or turning them against me, or even making me such a dangerous companion that no one in their right mind would stand beside me, then he had another think coming.

I was going to take the war to Cheapteeth— and I hoped his own sick friends would be standing right where I could get at them.

But I was going to save Jemini first, and I was going to do it at any cost. After all, apart from my friends, what else did I really have to lose?

SEVENTH MISTAKE:

ASKING THE WRONG QUESTIONS

The bed in Mrs. Looker's spare room was thin and narrow but seemed enormous when compared with the frail figure now lying in it.

Mrs. Looker and Evil Clive spent what felt like an age just staring at Jemini, neither of them giving a single opinion or word of helpful advice on the vampire girl's condition. Then they both retreated to another room amid a mutter of hushed conversation, while little Forgoth fetched a glass of water and tried to at least trickle some of the liquid into her mouth.

"Why aren't they helping?" I whispered to Max, trying not to sound as angry as I felt.

Max sighed. "Maybe they can't," he said. "I know I've never seen anything like it."

"But I thought you said that Clive—"

"Look, Ed. I don't know *everything*. I'm completely in the dark, and I'm guessing here as much as you are."

So we just waited while the clock on the wall ticked away some seemingly endless minutes, my flesh peeling off in small strips and Max slowly starting to stink the room out with his wet-doggy smell.

Eventually, Mrs. Looker emerged from the little room behind Evil Clive, who clicked across the floor to make another, more careful inspection of the wound on Jemini's neck. This time he picked at the puffy flesh around the bite, peered back at Mrs. Looker, and simply nodded.

Max and I glanced from one to the other, our fear mixing with anger as we patiently waited for some answers.

"It's a Liquid Curse," said the old gaunt, folding her arms. "Very old, very powerful, and practically impossible to remove."

"No way!" I felt my jaw drop open, but it wasn't a voluntary movement, so I snatched hold of my chin before it hit the floor. "That Stein woman's bites are cursed? How the heck—"

"No." Mrs Looker shook her head. "The bite simply ripped an opening in her neck: the curse was prepared beforehand in some sort of ritual and probably poured from a vial or injected with a syringe."

"A ritual?" I repeated. I risked a sideways glance at Max, who looked shocked and equally appalled. "In that case, maybe we—"

"Liquid Curses can't be reversed or lifted by any normal means," Clive interjected, his teeth clicking together as he talked. "The only way to shift a Liquid Curse is to destroy the one who created it . . . and I'm guessing that the most likely suspect is your nemesis: the clown. Remove him, and Jemini's recovery would be practically instantaneous."

I felt my jaw tighten, which came as a pleasant surprise.

This was all down to *Cheapteeth*.

"She's not dying because of *me*," I snarled,

"and I *mean* that . . . even if I have to crash the freaky circus and take on that sick clown single-handedly."

I wasn't joking. I would gladly have taken my own personal war to Midden Field, but the look on Max's face told me I wasn't going to have that choice . . . and even I'm not stupid enough to argue with an angry werewolf.

"Ed." The word had come from Evil Clive, and something about the skeleton's icy tone made both Max and me freeze to the spot. "You need to understand something. It's really not a good idea for you to be around Cheapteeth, whether you're intending to fight him . . . or not."

I frowned and shared a worried glance with Max. It seemed like a very *odd* thing to say. Clive must have thought so too because he put a bony hand on my shoulder and sighed. "I believe you are cursed in a way that might potentially make you as dangerous as Cheapteeth himself."

At first, the skeletal fingers distracted me from what Clive was saying. I wondered if this truly *was* my future—no skin, no muscle, no organs—just shiny white bone. It was only when his words echoed inside my head for a second time that I understood what he was talking about.

"You mean this, don't you?" We both looked down at my nine-fingered hand.

"Yes, Ed. I mean that." Evil Clive glanced back at Mrs. Looker, who was practically biting her nails with worry. "Let's just say that it's highly suspicious that the hand came back to you in the way it did . . . and we'll leave it at that. Be careful, Ed. Just make sure that *you* are always in control."

Apart from the stink of rotting flesh and the fact that bits of flesh and bone fell away from my body and I was physically repulsive to everyone I met, I guess being a zombie was preferable to being one of Mortlake's other undead citizens. At least it was the way Max told it.

"And then there are ghouls . . . don't even get me started."

He'd been talking for the better part of an hour as we lay in the half-dark of Mrs. Looker's wrecked basement, both wriggling uncomfortably on a couple of old, soggy mattresses.

So many thoughts were jostling for position in my head, but Evil Clive's voice continued to repeat the same ominous warning over and over again: *Just make sure that you are always in control.* But what did he mean? Could I actually *lose* possession of myself?

Did he mean just the rogue arm or my entire body? My...*soul*? I shuddered at the thought. I really couldn't bear thinking about it.

"And the ghasts...well, they're just a pair of legs and half a chin, really...."

Unbelievable. Max was *still* gabbing on. But not absolutely everything he'd said was entirely pointless...especially when it came to Jemini.

We'd been forbidden from leaving the house on Prospect Hill by Evil Clive, who'd decided that Jemini's fate was a community issue.

Max didn't agree, but nothing could have prepared me for the reason why. The astonishing fact he'd told me was still bouncing around inside my head, to the point where I couldn't really focus my attention on any of the disgusting stuff he'd told me since.

"Jemini is your SISTER?" I repeated, interrupting some hideous and strangely boring fact about ghouls eating corpses. "B-but how can she be? When you first introduced me to her, you just said she was a vampire! Evil Clive's second-in-command, you said!"

Max shrugged. "It's true: she bosses everyone around when Clive's busy … but she's still my sister, and that's why I'm not going to let anyone tell us we can't go after Cheapteeth on our own … even if it *is* Evil Clive."

"But I don't understand! Why didn't you tell me this before?"

Another shrug.

"It never came up. Besides . . . there's a reason we don't talk much about it. You know, painful memories and stuff."

The horror of the situation didn't dawn on me immediately, but—as I was lying in the dark, listening to the rain splashing through the floorboards above—the obvious truth suddenly hit me.

"Oh no—you were from the same family. That must have been awful . . . and not just for you: for your folks."

Max didn't say anything for a long time, and I wondered if I'd made him angry with such an obviously stupid statement.

"Jemini drowned in a lake when we were on a family holiday. It was icy, and we were being stupid. I tried to save her . . . but I . . . couldn't."

I let out a deep sigh, watching the stinky green mist that now passed for my breath as it hung in the air. To my surprise, it was my next question that seemed to cause Max the most distress.

"So did you die trying to save her?" I asked.

My werewolf friend sat up, sharp. His features were dark, and his eyes were filled with tears.

"Let's talk about something else," he muttered. "There's no point dwelling on the past. It's OVER."

"I just want to try to understand ... that's all."

Max put a hand to his face and didn't move it. For a moment I thought he might collapse in a fit of anguish, but he started to speak again ... and his voice was an empty pit of despair.

"Jemini died saving ME," he said, trying to stop himself from shaking as the memory resurfaced. "I was a bad kid, and I fell in with the wrong crowd. I was doing stupid stuff to try to impress them. Then things got out of hand. One day, we were out to steal a bike, but then two of the older kids stole a car instead. I didn't want to go with them, but I didn't have the guts to stand up to them. Jemini tried to stop me. We had a bad accident, and they rolled the car into a lake. We all got out ... but Jemini ..."

"Didn't." I finished the sentence for Max but felt so sad looking at him that I didn't know what to say or do.

I was about to apologize for bringing up such a painful subject when a noise from the floor above caused us both to jump.

"What was—"

Max coughed and dried his eyes.

"Mrs. Looker's just gone to bed," he muttered. "That's our cue: we're leaving."

I watched as Max leapt to his feet and grabbed for the backpack he'd spent so much of the evening filling with assorted supplies.

"Now listen, Ed," he muttered, sniffing the air as if some dusty cloud in the cellar could give him the latest news from all over town. "Mrs. Looker has put a field around the house to stop us from leaving, so we're going to have to go via the sewer. I'm sure I don't need to remind you how dangerous it's likely to be. . . ."

I shook my head. Nothing except a total mind-wipe would ever remove *those* memories.

He mooched over to the middle of the room and dragged back one of the mattresses, revealing an old and half-crumbled wooden trapdoor.

"I also need to ask you a big favor," he went on, wrenching up the wooden portal and splashing into the murky darkness.

I took one last glance around the basement and followed him down.

"Anything," I said. "You can ask me for any—"

"I need that big gut you've got flopping over your trousers, there."

We both looked down. At least Max had the decency to look slightly embarrassed.

I'd never been what you would call fat, but my ever-so-slightly fleshy stomach was still largely intact. It was hanging over my jeans a bit, but not much.

"You want this?" I said, nervously gripping a hand- ful and squeez- ing it between my thumb and what was left of one forefinger.

"Yeah. It's for the ghouls. The

ones in the sewers are wild beyond belief—we need something to distract them. Er ... sorry, dude."

I looked down and gulped back a burp of disgust. Then I closed my eyes, grabbed a handful of my own flab, and tugged. It came away and hit the ground with a sickening plop . . . as my own voice echoed inside my head.

You better get used to this, Ed. If Evil Clive really is a zombie, you might as well let go of some fat now before it all just falls away. . . .

Max scooped up the fleshy slice. "That should be enough, buddy. Thanks."

Ten minutes later, we were both proceeding at a decent pace through the sewer, Max stopping every few seconds to break off a piece of my gut and sling it along one of the many side tunnels.

"Keeps them hunting in all the *wrong* places," he explained. "You've done us a great favor. Try not to keep thinking about it."

Nice words . . . but they were easier said than done . . . especially since I could now see a small section of my own pelvis. Fortunately, a distant roar shifted my concentration.

"What the hell was that?" I spluttered, suddenly darting glances down every new junction as Max headed purposefully down the central passage. "Ghouls?"

Max shook his head, and I noticed that his arm hair had begun to bristle. We both increased our pace, but a second roar—still far off but definitely closer than the first—spurred Max into a healthy sprint.

I tried my best to keep up, but I had my work cut out. It was like trying to match speed with a guy on horseback.

"Let me guess," I panted, as we booked it down several new tunnels. "There's a big daddy ghoul that's twice the size of all the others."

Max laughed. "I wish. The thing that's following us is called Mush, and it would make a ghoul daddy look like a baby hamster."

"Seriously?"

"Seriously."

I prayed to the gods that Max was lying,

exaggerating, maybe even pulling my leg. But he wasn't . . . and I know that because we ran into the thing known as Mush on the next bend.

To this day, I can scarcely describe it. . . .

EIGHTH MISTAKE:

BEING IN THE WRONG PLACE AT THE WRONG TIME

When you see something terrible, something hideous, something so out of your comfort zone that your skin itches and your heart thumps out of your chest, it is not unusual for a strange state of heightened awareness to take over your body.

It happened to me, because Mush was quite literally an assault on the senses. I could see him, but I honestly had no idea what I was looking at; I could hear him, but the buzzing set my teeth on edge; I could smell him . . . and that nearly killed me all over again.

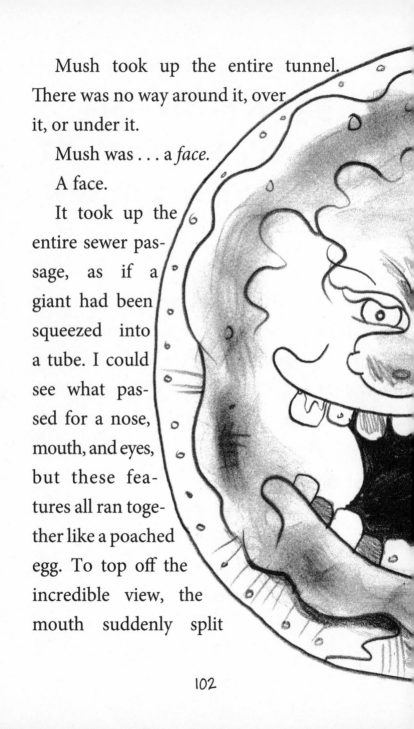

Mush took up the entire tunnel. There was no way around it, over it, or under it.

Mush was . . . a *face*.

A face.

It took up the entire sewer passage, as if a giant had been squeezed into a tube. I could see what passed for a nose, mouth, and eyes, but these features all ran together like a poached egg. To top off the incredible view, the mouth suddenly split

open, revealing black and yellow teeth the size of fence posts.

"Run," Max growled, backing up quickly. "He's going to spew! RUUUUUN!"

I turned on my heels, but not fast enough.

Mush opened his enormous mouth and vomited a billowing cloud of gas in our direction. It hurtled down the tunnel at an incredible speed, finally triggering the panic inside my stomach to spur me away.

I splashed back to the junction and stopped dead. Max was nowhere to be seen.

I wanted to call out to him, but the roar that erupted from behind me would have drowned out whatever I tried to shout. An intense buzzing filled my ears as the green cloud spilled from the mouth of the tunnel I'd just left.

I glanced both ways and opted for the tunnel on my right, hoping it might also have

been Max's choice. I threw all my might into a determined sprint for the end but slipped on the slimy under path and fell face-first into the murky waters of the main sewer river.

Trying desperately not to breathe in any of the hideous lumps that floated in the filthy wash like crackers in a soup, I propelled myself back to the sidewalk, clambering onto the slippery path and almost sliding off again

as I squinted to see along the tunnel I was trying to negotiate.

Then all at once I was embroiled in a complete nightmare.

Three wild ghouls appeared at the junction with the next tunnel, their eyes glowing red and their tiny mouths salivating with savage hunger. Each one was a pale but fleshy blob

with wobbling, sack-like folds of skin, and they moved deceptively fast. Two were crawling along the passage walls at a heavy pace, while the third scurried across the roof of the tunnel.

I tried to retrace my steps ... but there was Mush, its enormous face shadowed in another swath of swirling cloud.

The roar, this time, was deafening, a wild, primal boom of sound ... but it only seemed to stop one of the ghouls from advancing. The other two had evidently decided that their hunger was more important than their safety and came scampering toward me even faster than before.

I did some quick, on-the-spot calculations in my head and came up with the following options.

One: Run forward, fight the ghouls, and most likely end up shredded into ribbons.

Two: Run backward, get eaten by Mush, partially digested, and then probably plopped out in some subterranean sewer pipe with anything else it might have recently eaten.

Three: Stay where I was, get shredded by the ghouls, and *then* eaten by Mush.

I was still trying to think of a fourth option when a tidal wave of puke exploded from the giant, pulsating head and swept down the tunnels like an angry sea, blasting into me with the unswerving force of a major hurricane.

I gulped, then cried out, then spat. I was determined not to swallow any of the rancid vomit.

"Arghghghghggh!"

The stink of fish guts and puke was completely engulfing. I was turned over and over in the water like a fish caught in a swirling whirlpool.

I tried to swim away, but fate had it in for me ... and I was dashed against the side of the tunnel.

I smacked my head hard on the sidewalk just as the monster attacked.

The world became a mass of blurred images I knew I'd rather not see. As the first ghoul was bitten in half and the sewer wall sprayed with a shower of fresh blood, I began to lose consciousness.

My last thought before Mush devoured the remaining ghouls and the horrible green waters of the river closed over my head was *I wonder what happened to Max.*

Then I was carried away on the tide of vomit, and everything went dark.

Waking up in a nice warm bed is lovely. Waking up on a wet bed in a cold room is not so lovely but still—in the scheme of things—kinda okay.

Waking up in a stinking, filthy sewer is neither lovely nor kinda okay, and waking up *at the bottom of the sewer river* needs a whole new definition ... because, sadly, VOMITIZA-TION isn't yet recognized as a proper word.

It should be.

The world was a gloomy emerald color, and this was because I'd sunk to the bottom of a green river in a waterway pumped with green chemicals. I felt like a really sick little fish in a pond next to a nuclear power plant.

To make matters worse, something long and thin floated past me . . . and there were corn kernels in it.

I've never moved so fast in my life.

I practically grew gills to swim out of that river.

When I surfaced, there was no sign of the ghouls or Mush, and—thankfully—a distant roar signaled that the latter was now some way off.

"Max!" I called in a frantic sort of half-whisper. "Max! Can you hear me?"

Nothing. I was angry and frustrated. I still

couldn't believe the ragged little fur ball had blown me off in order to save his own shaggy hide.

I stomped off down the west tunnel, keeping to the walkway and trying to mutter under my breath. I decided to turn left at every new junction, which seemed like a great idea until I passed the same rotting fish carcass twice.

Alternating lefts and rights worked much better . . . especially when I rounded a bend to find Max halfway up a ladder.

"About time!" he said upon catching sight of me. "Quick! Help me with this manhole cover!"

I glared up at him.

"I wouldn't help you pick your own nose, you flea-bitten mutt! You left me here alone!"

Max grinned, flashing his elongated teeth as he returned his attention to the cover.

"I told you to run! I can't babysit you through everything, you know."

"*Babysit* me?"

"Yeah . . . besides, Mush would probably have spat you out anyway. You smell almost as bad as he does, and even eaters have *some* taste."

He burst out laughing as I snatched hold of the lower rungs and began to climb.

"I'd hurry up if I were you, Ed. Judging by that last roar, he's on his way back."

"Then maybe we should keep the noise down—"

Max ignored me and started to hammer on the manhole cover above.

"We must be on the outskirts by now!" he said, between strikes. "C'mon, QUICK!"

The cover finally gave way, and Max rolled out into the moonlight. I hurtled after him, and together we managed to haul the great disk back into its slot. Then a rumble beneath us shook the ground, and Max and I tripped as we tried to get to our feet.

"What is that thing?" I managed, clinging to the ground while the thundering chaos continued beneath me. The noise was worse than a subway train at rush hour.

Max blew out a puff of cold night air. "Mush used to be an eater," he said.

"Like Tom?"

"Yeah, in the beginning . . . but he got trapped in the sewer and grew long instead of out. Now he's just this massive length of flesh, like a giant snake with a big human face."

"Big isn't the word." I shuddered. "Did you see that gas he threw up?"

"That wasn't gas!" Max laughed. "That was a swarm of tiny flies. They live in his teeth, clinging to the bits of corpses that stick to the gums."

I felt sick.

Physically sick.

The full moon was keeping a watchful eye over the nocturnal landscape of Mortlake. It bathed the edge of the forest in a pale wash of evening light.

"We'll keep to the woods," Max suggested, already heading off toward the first line of trees. "Less chance of a bad encounter in there...."

We entered the woods and I noticed with some relief that Max immediately found the best trail. He must have known this place like the back of his hand: he didn't even need to hit the ground for a sniff.

"This way. It's pretty much a straight route from the north side of the wood to Midden Field. Don't you remember?"

I nodded vaguely, but the truth was I *didn't* remember much from my old life . . . and I was forgetting more and more every day. It started with little things, like the layout of the town and a few street names I couldn't quite recall, then progressed to faces from my past and random memories that didn't seem clear in my head. It was frightening, and the older stuff was disappearing fast, as if my memory was one long escalator being chewed up from the bottom. I wondered how long it would be before I forgot my favorite times at school, or even—and this I couldn't bear thinking about—the faces of my parents.

I could feel the sadness swallowing me up, and even though I tried everything not to dwell on it, my mind raced away.

No more memories...

Was this all part of becoming empty...like Clive? Was this the weird journey from zombie to walking, talking skeleton ... and what then? What happened afterward? Was Clive on some dark, twisting path that would see him end up as a forgotten prop in a science lab?

"You okay?" Max asked, as we continued to trudge along the frosty path. "You look a bit...funny."

"I was just thinking about stuff, that's all. I know this probably happens to everyone who dies, but—"

"I was talking about your eye."

"My what?"

I raised a hand to my face and—almost dreading what I might feel—touched my eye socket with my fingers. Thankfully, nothing felt particularly out of the ordinary.

"Are you kidding me?" I asked Max.

The werewolf shook his head. "Not really, dude. Your right eyeball has slipped a bit: it's looking down toward your cheek."

"Rubbish."

"I'm *serious*."

To test out this grim observation, I closed my left eye and looked just out of the right one.

The view was pretty bleak: all I could see was the forest path and a pink border where my cheek must have been.

ONE

"You're right; I can only see the floor."

This is ridiculous, I thought. *How am I supposed to have any sort of afterlife in this condition? If the other eye goes the same way, I'm toast.*

Max sighed. "You're in big trouble if the other one checks out, too," he muttered, reading my worried expression. "Unless it flips upward: at least then you've got everything covered."

"Yeah," I agreed. *What a comforting thought.*

"Don't sweat it," Max said, giving me a friendly pat. "Clive doesn't have any eyeballs, and he still seems to see okay. Mind you, I did once hear him say that he could only ever feel stuff, not exactly s—"

"OKAY, OKAY! STOP TALKING, WILL YOU? YOU'RE NOT HELPING." I gritted my teeth and rolled what was left of my eyes.

NINTH MISTAKE:

JUST CHARGING IN

Midden Field was usually a dark, forgotten wilderness on the outskirts of town. You might see a pile of trash there from time to time, or the occasional cow, but—mostly—it was one of Mortlake's old and forgotten farming grounds.

Until now. . . .

The place was alive with lights: red, green, blue, purple, yellow. It was like watching the world's biggest and most prolonged firework display. There were flashing, eerily illuminated signs everywhere . . . and something told me they weren't being powered by electricity: a crackle of dark and powerful energy ran along the outline of every tent.

Most carnival setups are composed of a number of separate tents, kiosks, and stands—whereas Carble and Stein's ghostly circus consisted of a vast, sprawling network of brightly covered canvas marquees, all streaming out from the central big top as if the enormously distorted core had grown a variety of spindly limbs.

"It's massive," Max whispered from our hiding place on the edge of the wood. "Where do you think Cheapteeth and his cronies are? The big top?"

I shrugged. "They might be, but—well— we don't know, do we? Those demons must all be in there somewhere, too. I've got a bad feeling about this. Maybe we should have waited for Clive and the others."

Max took a deep breath but appeared to be steeling himself for the change. I could see the full moon reflected in his eyes.

"It's time," he growled. "Let's go."

I followed him down the incline and onto the edge of the field, swearing when I stepped in some ghostly dog doo despite having one eye firmly on the grass. Even though it was

little more than a wisp of spirit grossness, I still couldn't shake it off the end of my foot without jumping up and down three or four times.

There were about a hundred different entrances to Carble and Stein's bizarre circus, and all the signs were in some strange language I couldn't understand.

"It's Arcanum," Max whispered.

"Arcanum?"

"Demon language: Evil Clive can read it."

"I wish we could."

"Yeah, me too."

To say the place was weird would have been a dramatic understatement. All the usual circus stands and stalls were present, but none of them were manned and all of them had some twisted, sickening element that I have never seen in any *living* circus I'd ever visited.

The dunking booth had a half-rotted human

corpse perched on the end, barely supported over a container of what looked and smelled like blood. The Whac-A-Ghoul game urged you to bop a collection of shrunken ghoul heads, all with one sewn-up eye mimicking the look of Jessica Stein, while the ring toss involved trying to throw a series of tied intestinal cords over the top of various decapitated limbs that sprouted from the floor.

"I hate this place already," Max whispered. "And we haven't even gone in yet."

I peered around with equal disgust, but an even darker feeling was stealing over me. "It's too quiet here. I can't help but get the feeling that we're walking into a trap."

Looking back, I have to wonder what might have happened to us had Max not suddenly tripped on a block of wood half lodged in the base of one of the sideshow stalls.

"Argh! What the hell—"

I crouched beside my werewolf friend, intending to haul him back to his feet, when I spotted a solitary demon flying low over an outlying field to the west.

"Shh!" I urged Max. "Stay down!"

We both hunkered against the flapping canvas walls of the stall, watching with bated breath as the demon—one of the little monstrosities from Stein's attack on Prospect

Hill—came in for a landing on the edge of the Midden ground and promptly scampered for a brightly colored tunnel that opened in the shape of a gaping yellow mouth.

"In there! Quick!"

We dashed across the open ground, weaving our way between the stalls and trying to stay as low as we could.

By the time we arrived at the giant mouth, the little demon was a tiny receding dot at the end of the corridor. It paused for a second, then flittered off to the left.

Max glanced up briefly at the moon, and his hair began to rise.

We both steeled ourselves and hurried inside.

Despite my determination to seem like I was firmly in control, a dark wave of fear was washing over me. Taking on Kambo Cheapteeth in any circumstances was a terrible step into the unknown, but on his home turf it would be like striking a match in a gunpowder factory. I was absolutely, completely terrified.

Fortunately, I didn't have time to dwell on my fear.

"Haaahahaahahaahahahahahahahah!"

A cacophony of sickening laughter echoed all around the interior of the canvas maze as we forged our way ahead. It sounded as though the stream of noise was being played on a loop, because several of the same snorts and giggles seemed to signal the end of each batch. Either way, it was creeping Max out; he seemed to be stuck in a sort of half-wolf shape, and I knew that only happened when a particular fear was gripping him.

The fork where the demon turned was well lit, but there was absolutely no sign of the little fiend. Following its route to the left, I was disappointed when we hit yet another intersection, especially when there were three possible exits.

"It could have gone anywhere," Max whispered.

I shook my head, trying to figure out where we were in relation to the big top. It was difficult to think; the laughter was getting louder and louder. The sheer lunacy of it burrowed under my skin and set my nerves on edge.

Max narrowed his eyes and squinted along

the central passage. "We should go straight ahead," he muttered. "I can see someone moving, up there. Look!"

He suddenly shifted up a gear, making a determined dash for the end of the corridor. I couldn't see what he was looking at, but then I had only the one good eye, and he could probably command an entire army of wolf senses, so naturally I followed him.

About halfway along the passage, he stopped dead, crouched, and began to snarl in the low, guttural tone I'd come to recognize as his threatening growl.

Now I could see the movement in front of Max . . . but something about it alerted me to the fact that the shadow wasn't an enemy at all.

Every circus has a hall of mirrors.

"Max! Hold up. It's your reflection, you doughnut!"

But the wolf in Max wasn't too sure. The growling continued as I made my way past him and stood between the two, waving my hand in front of the glass.

It *was* a good mirror, I have to admit . . . and disguised so well that you couldn't actually see the edges.

Beyond it, a well-lit maze led off in all directions. The bright light was matched only by the million images cast around the walls, reflecting, distorting, and stretching my disgusting appearance to infinity.

"Do we have to go in there?" Max growled. "I'm likely to be really jumpy, and you might get your head clawed off or something. . . ."

I glanced back the way we'd come and shrugged.

"It *does* go in the direction of the big top," I admitted. "Besides, we're both dead. What's the worst that can happen?"

Max glared at me, and I just knew he was thinking about Jemini and her screaming purple agony.

"Yeah," I said, reluctantly. "Apart from that."

TENTH MISTAKE:

TAKING A GOOD, LONG LOOK AT MYSELF

The hall of mirrors in any circus is a weird and freaky place. Each length of glass shows your image contorted any number of ways: fat, thin, tall, short, wide, angled . . . you name it. You get to glimpse the reflection you see every day morphed into something terrible.

Then your friends start laughing, you tag along, and within seconds, the whole episode has become hilarious and you're having the time of your life.

That's in a normal circus.

The hall of mirrors at Carble and Stein's

uniquely creepy carnival didn't stretch us or shrink us or even turn us upside down. What it did was much worse.

It brought us back to life.

I stood watching myself in better days as I went off to school. I was happy, smiling, laughing, and joking with two friends who I was shocked to realize I didn't even recognize.

Then, suddenly, the image in the mirror flashed and flickered and the past became the future. My reflection beamed as it raised a hand to its head and began peeling away the skin. In an instant, I was looking at a grinning human skeleton.

My eyes filled with tears, and I was angry, because I couldn't help it. At least the emotion gave me the strength to pull my gaze away from the vision.

I shook my head and wiped the tears from my ragged cheeks.

Max, standing a short distance away, seemed to be equally horrified. When I managed to pull myself away from my own grinning reflection I saw why he was so upset.

The Max in the mirror didn't look any-thing like my undead mate. In fact, it looked so *unlike* him that for a moment, I thought it was someone else.

Then I noticed a quirky crease around the jawline and a slight lean to the smirk-ing mouth. It was definitely Max . . . but he seemed so different: less hollow, more ener-getic, more . . . alive!

"They've deliberately done this to upset us," I snapped, grabbing hold of Max and dragging him away from the image. "Let's just keep moving. All the while we're hang-ing around this dump, Jemini isn't getting any better."

We ran on, trying to ignore our haunt-ing pasts as they flashed on and off from the walls on all sides. The insane laughter, piped throughout the circus, was now set at an almost ear-splitting volume.

136

Round and round and round we ran, up one corridor, down another, left at the first set of mirrors, straight ahead at the next. It was no use: this place redefined the word *maze*.

"How do we get out of here?" Max growled, covering his ears as the single cackle of laughter from the lunatic speaker brought him closer to the edge of madness. "I can't even see where we came in."

"That's the point of a maze," I muttered, equally annoyed but trying to think. "The only thing you can do in a place like this is something they don't *expect* you to do. . . ."

"Such as?"

"Well . . . how about . . . THIS?"

I took a run up and booted one of the mirrors. It exploded on impact and showered us both with a million tiny shards of glass.

There was a larger passageway behind it, and
the entire area seemed to open out a lot more.

Max turned to me with an expansive grin and muttered, "I like your style."

We both took a determined step forward and entered the next part of the circus.

I'd always assumed that Kambo Cheapteeth knew about the world of the dead long before he joined it. Anyone crazy enough to commit suicide in the name of some arcane god and talk two other morons into doing the same was either deeply, deeply disturbed or just plain crazy. Either way, I'm guessing that Cheapteeth didn't exactly get his wish: spending all of eternity as a demented, ugly, putrefying clown cannot have been what he bargained for when he scrawled his magic symbols in the back of his carnival trailer. Personally, if I had been given a choice, I'd have gone for not dying (and maybe a really hot girlfriend, forty million in gold coins, and an Xbox Kinect).

Despite all this, Cheapteeth must have harnessed *some* sort of magical ability after his death. Otherwise, this circus base of his couldn't have existed ...

... and exist it DID.

The weird, twisted corridors reminded me of the hideouts occupied by Batman villains in that series my dad used to watch: all slanted floors and ceilings. To make things even more unsettling, TV screens were suspended on the walls at odd angles, playing sick cartoons that definitely weren't Sunday afternoon entertainment.

"This place is warped," Max said, watching the mouse in the animation slowly sewing up the eyeballs of its feline enemy. "Let's just find Cheapteeth, rip him apart, and then get the heck out of here."

I nodded ahead as we rounded a twist in the passage. "Can't imagine it's going to be that easy."

There, at the far end of the next corridor, was a set of red, yellow, and purple curtains fastened back with a length of white rope. Beyond, the massive expanse of the big top beckoned...

...and there wasn't an empty seat in the house.

ELEVENTH MISTAKE:

BITING OFF MORE THAN I COULD CHEW

I was never so grateful to be in the shadows as my eyes took in the scene.

Nightmare City.

The big top was *packed* with demons.

A sea of red waved, chattered, and fidgeted around the walls as Max and I stared, open-mouthed at the incredible interior of the circus's core. Amid crowded coils of seating lay the vast arena stage, a white circle bathed in the glare of what seemed like a hundred unseen spotlights. There, center stage, stood the filthy, brass-toothed midget we all now knew to be the erstwhile Vincent Carble. Cheapteeth's right-hand man was wedged between two enormous lions that each looked capable of devouring him without a second thought. They weren't ordinary circus animals by any stretch of the imagination: both had rotting flesh, exposed bones, and the twisted, blood-shot eyes of the cursed. Above this diorama of concentrated evil, the floating form of Jessica Stein was visible at one end of a tightrope that spanned the roof of the big top. She drifted aimlessly back and forth, spitting out demented cackles and waving her arms at random.

"Where is he getting all these *things* from?" I muttered, gripping Max's arm tight when he tried to take a step forward. "I mean, he just died like the rest of us, right?"

"He died *cursed*."

"So did I."

Max turned to me. "No, Ed. You *were* cursed. Cheapteeth cursed himself. When that happens, sometimes you attract ... attention."

"From who?"

"Forget it. Let's just say he's obviously getting help from a very powerful frien—"

Max stopped talking as the spotlight hit us.

The light was unbearable: a searing, burning white pool of blistering intensity that threw us into sharp focus while the rest of the big top was plunged into shadow.

"Ah ..." said a voice that sounded like it came from the depths of evil. "Our shtar turn hash arrived. A big round of applaushe, pleashe—for our honored guest, the ever-decomposhing Edward Bagley."

144

An explosion of thunderous clapping ripped into our ears as a second spotlight relit the stage. Kambo Cheapteeth staggered down a twisted spiral walkway where each step seemed to appear only a fraction of a second before he arrived upon it. The clown,

clad head to toe in festering, half-torn, over-
sized clothes, was speaking into a strange ice
cream cone that seemed to be both amplifying
and distorting his dark, syrupy voice, streaming it around the arena as his army of servants
chattered in the background.

Max bristled to life, his bones and teeth
elongating, his jaw extending and hair sprouting in full glory from his nose, ears, and arms.

Within seconds, I was standing beside a giant werewolf. Max, it seemed, had a super-strength button concealed somewhere about his person . . . and it had been firmly pressed.

I felt like a ferret standing next to a walrus.

"Impresshive," crowed the jellied voice of Cheapteeth. "But I fear you'll need shlightly more than one big mutt to have any chanche of leaving this plache with whatsh left of your organsh. Don't feel bad, Ed—you'd never have eshcaped my clutchesh even if you'd brought along *all* your friendsh . . . you were doomed the moment you *interfered* in my death."

My hand began to twitch at my side.

"It's not my fault your crazy suicide went wrong, Cheapteeth," I screamed back at the clown. "Now just tell us which of your pathetic minions cursed Jemini so Max and I can wipe it out and get on with the rest of our deaths."

"Whahahaahahah!"

The laughter went on and on for what seemed like an age, and I felt Max getting ready to race for the stage. Something was holding my werewolf friend back, probably the same edge of icy fear that prevented me from advancing.

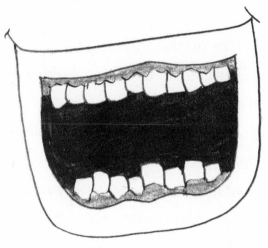

"Shorry to dishappoint you, Ed . . . but, in fact, my shuichide went almost exactly according to plan," came the booming voice once more, stifling another round of maniacal laughter. "But you, shadly, *were* in the

148

wrong plache at the worsht posshible time ...
and now I require your shoul's complete desh-
truction in order to give mine ... full power."

And, suddenly, there it was: Kambo Cheapteeth needed my spirit in order to charge
up his own ... like he was a flashlight and I
was a set of AA batteries. Nice. Still, at least
it explained why the demented lunatic had
hunted me down.

The clown was still talking, but his words
weren't getting any clearer. ...

"Letsh not jusht shtand around all day ...
let ush have shome *fun* before we draw our
show to a grand finale. The cursh you sheek to
lift came from none other than my eshteemed
colleague, Mishter Carble. Let's shee if you
can get to him, shall we?"

Max didn't hesitate. Howling with insane
fury, he sprang down the central aisle and
tore toward Carble. Unfortunately, the two
undead lions ripped forward at the same pace,

and both collided with Max in the middle of the circle.

Carble grinned, his brass teeth flashing in the glint of the spotlight, and scampered off toward a rickety ladder that spanned the gap between the floor and Stein's arcing tightrope.

My hand twitched again, and I was off.

Expecting the sea of demons to pour over me at any moment like a school of piranhas, I closed one eye to steady my balance and ran, desperately trying to circumnavigate the fight between Max and the lions as I made for the foot of the ladder.

For some reason, it worried me even more when no attack was made. The screeching, squealing ocean of imps just watched the show as the spotlight followed my progress in the chase.

Carble was moving at incredible speed for such a short-limbed man, climbing the ladder like a spider monkey and then swinging underneath the tightrope before advancing along it.

Stein swooped in to protect the scurrying midget, looking every inch the spider queen fiercely guarding her young.

I was closing in on the pair and had just reached the top of the ladder when my ever-failing body chose the most catastrophic moment to let go of a major asset.

My foot dropped off.

DROPPED off.

I felt a lightness underneath me and then watched with horror as the entire foot simply pitched away into the gloom.

A cacophony of grim laughter deafened my senses.

"Bad luck there, Ed. I didn't know it would be shoe eashy to make you looshe your shole. Shole, get it? Hahaha! I'm shuch a heel! Whahahaha-hah!"

I gritted my teeth and balanced precariously on one leg. I was going to have to cross the tightrope on *one* leg.

Insane.

My hand twitched again, and, before I could stop myself, I was moving along the tightrope. It was starting to feel like part of my brain was actually embedded in the freaky fingers; despite expelling the Cheapteeth parasite from the arm, I seemed to have very little control over my own movement. As if to underline this thought, I tried to take a step backward ... but it didn't happen.

It was the most pathetic tightrope walk in history.

I took several strangely controlled steps forward, regained control of my senses, and fell.

The hand flicked up like a cobra and snatched hold of the line.

I dangled like a fly on a strand of web, part of me wanting to let go while the rest of me screamed an order not to look down.

Unfortunately, I had no choice ... because my *bad* eyelid fluttered open.

Far below, on the arena floor, Max was being circled by the two undead lions. Despite the size of the three creatures, they looked like miniatures when viewed from such a height.

I wanted to help Max—he certainly looked like he would *need* help against the pair of rotting big cats, but the hand had other ideas.

I'd barely had time to breathe before I was vaulted upward once more. I shot into the air like a poisoned dart, hung around the circus roof as my descent slowed, and then plummeted back to the wire.

My landing caused a ripple on the line that made Jessica Stein take to the air once more. Even Carble, who was holding the wire with both hands and feet, scampered for the safety of the far platform.

I looked down and gasped with shock as my body began to move of its own accord. A sickening crack from my remaining foot echoed around the big top as the bones divided and folded around the wire. I felt sick. My foot was now a boneless flesh maw and had fastened onto the line with an unearthly determination…like an old man's false teeth clasping a chewy sweet. Even a hurricane wouldn't have shifted me from the wire.…

I was propelled downward and cried out with surprise as I was pulled flat to the line, my demon hand grasping the wire.

Then, accompanied by a deafening roar that I couldn't quite believe had originated from my own lips, the hand twisted around the wire and pulled.

No, not pulled: wrenched…with the strength of an army.

It brought down the entire scaffold, sending both platforms and the wire between them crashing to the circus floor.

Unfortunately for Jessica Stein, her midget friend had sensed the danger and leapt at her feet for safety, dragging her to the floor along with everything else. On the way down, she became tangled in the wire's safety netting, kicking free of the midget as she fought to escape.

Max and his two savage opponents were swallowed up in the debris that mushroomed up from the fallout of the collapse.

The big top was suddenly a bowl of heavy darkness, with only a single erratic spotlight dancing over the shadows apparently at random.

I hit the ground like Humpty Dumpty . . . and ended up in roughly the same condition.

Don't get me wrong—I *knew* my body was weakening. What I didn't know was that one hard impact would send me spinning to the four winds.

CRUNCH.

Bear in mind that I only saw this from my one good eye in the sporadic illumination of the single darting spotlight. But I can still put the full picture together. Unfortunately.

My head snapped away from my spinal

column and rolled into the corner of the circle like a really well-kicked soccer ball.

It's impossible to describe what it looks and feels like when your head rolls away. All you can see is the floor and the ceiling, spinning in a kaleidoscope of weirdness until you eventually bounce to a halt. Thankfully, I landed facing the circle, otherwise what happened afterward would have been anyone's guess.

At least I got to see my foot again: the one that had fallen from the tightrope platform was now three centimeters from my bad eyeball.

The demon hand ripped away immediately, scurrying into the darkness and taking most of the left arm with it. I wasn't really shocked at that. I'd only just gotten used to having it around in the first place.

That left my main body, which broke into two different pieces: the upper torso with my one remaining arm, and the midsection, complete with a partially functioning pair of legs (admittedly minus one foot).

I didn't have time to get over the shock of losing so many body bits before I realized with even greater surprise that I could still *feel* them.

I gritted my teeth as I urged my legs to get to their one remaining foot. They did, blundering around as more and more of the ghostly spotlights flooded back into the arena.

One of the lions had been speared by the collapsing scaffold. It pawed ineffectually at the ground but had been completely impaled and was becoming increasingly insubstantial: it now looked like nothing more than a child's drawing of a beast.

Unfortunately, the other creature was anything but destroyed, and it erupted from a haphazard pile of metal supports, roaring with rage and confusion.

A short distance away, Max emerged from an equally sturdy heap of wooden struts, looking slightly less alert than he had earlier. There were nasty wounds in his chest and legs, and something about the way he stalked forward suggested that he was slightly dazed. The lion barreled into him, and the battling pair rolled over and over as they each tried to land savage bites on the other. Flesh began to fly.

I shut my bad eye and tried to focus. My brain-link with the demon hand was practically nonexistent, but I did manage to convince my right arm to make its way toward me, dragging my upper torso with it.

Then Carble appeared. The little midget clawed his way from beneath the remains of a broken trapeze, his brass teeth gritted as spit flew from his lips. Reaching out with both hands, he snatched hold of my lower back—his grotesquely overgrown nails dug into my flesh and stopped my body's slow progress across the arena floor.

I winced as the pain of the attack resounded in my hindbrain.

"Get off me, you stinking, putrid, spit-faced gnome!" I yelled, concentrating all my focus on the torso and commanding my right arm to fight back. To my delight, the limb swung around and smacked the midget squarely in the face: once, twice, three times. I was about to utter a celebratory cheer when Carble bit hold of my hand on the last pass, sinking his gleaming teeth into the palm.

The pain took me all the way from mad to furious, and suddenly I knew just what to do.

Pursing my lips with the effort of concentration, I got my wandering legs to run at the wriggling midget.

Even with a missing foot, the legs responded well. Guided by my newly sharpened mind, they half hobbled, half hopped to the aid of my struggling torso, leaped into the air, and landed with a decisive stomp on the midget's fat little face.

To this day, I can still hear the *crack* as Carble's nose shattered.

Max and the lion were literally tearing strips off each other, but it appeared that the werewolf was now getting the best of the fight.

Using curved claws like eagle talons and teeth that were barely housed inside his elongated jaw, Max launched a final, deadly assault on the beast, going straight for the big cat's throat. The lion gave a demented roar and collapsed, but in doing so tore such a savage wound in Max's side that the werewolf collapsed and began to convulse violently on the floor.

I surveyed the situation, which looked worse for Mortlake Massive with every new second. It wasn't about to get any better. . . .

A bloodied hand reached down and snatched a handful of my hair, lifting my head from the ground.

My vision soared upward as the circus dropped away, and I just knew it was Jessica Stein holding my decapitated head.

All at once we landed on the outer circle of the Big Top's highest row of stalls. Surrounded by crowding demons, I was marched over to the gangly, cackling form of Kambo Cheapteeth, who bowed and gratefully accepted my head as if it was a nicely wrapped Christmas present from an elderly aunt.

I was abruptly turned to face the middle of the big top, as a fresh flood of light illuminated the clamoring interior. Jessica Stein flew down to aid Carble, who was barely conscious. She dragged him back onto his chubby feet.

"I'm sorry we never met in life, Ed," Cheapteeth whispered, his gnarled and yellowing teeth mere centimeters from my good eye. "I think we would have been great friends. Now …"

The clown took a deep breath, used his other hand to raise the twisted microphone to his disgusting lips, and bellowed. "Stein! Carble! Destroy the werewolf. My demons are hungry!"

"Stop! No! Please! Nooooooooooooo,"
I yelled out in frustrated desperation as the
hovering witch and her midget collaborator
grasped a length of scaffolding between them
and drove the pole deep into Max's heart.

At least, that's what they would have done
if the side of the big top hadn't suddenly gaped
open at that very moment, ripped asunder by
the gargantuan hands of Ten Tow Tom.

Demons screamed in fury, taking to the
skies and rolling over one another to escape

the clutches of the eater as it rumbled through the newly ripped gap in the canvas and barreled into the stalls, smashing the wooden seating into splinters.

A combined force of werewolves and vampires charged in the wake of the behemoth, attacking demons left and right as the creatures rallied to mount an offensive of their own.

Stein and Carble immediately halted their attempt to kill Max Moon and directed their attention to the ambush, which intensified with the arrival of Forgoth the Cursed and his free-roaming demonic entity, Mumps. Now in the form of an enormous mutant that appeared to be a cross between a tree and a teddy bear, Mumps carved a path toward the middle of the big top in an effort to offer Max some much needed protection.

When Evil Clive finally appeared, wearing his trademark raincoat with a baseball cap turned back to front on his skull, I was already on the move.

Kambo Cheapteeth, it seemed, had no desire to hang around for a confrontation with the undead hordes of the Mortlake Massive. Instead, he was leaving. Fast. And still holding on to my head.

"Heeelllp!" I yelled as each new level of the stalls rushed past at an impossible speed. In those frantic few seconds, I saw many things that were almost too terrible to describe . . . even if they were perpetrated by my own friends.

I saw Mumps snatch hold of Jessica Stein and rip her to pieces, stomping and crushing the bits that were left over.

I saw Max Moon stagger to his feet, still clutching the terrible wound in his side, and dropkick Vincent Carble into the waiting arms of the eater, who crunched him with a sound like someone working their way through a bag of sour cream and onion potato chips.

The demons took to the skies and fled.

And then I saw Evil Clive in pursuit, closing in on us as we disappeared from the big top and ran through the maze of canvas tunnels.

I fought to mentally connect with my increasingly disparate body but to no avail. On and on we went, as the canvas tunnels gave way to Midden Field and the circus became nothing more than a wash of eerie light in the distance.

Evil Clive vanished into mist and shadow as Kambo ran faster and faster, his great boots hitting the grass between leaps. The deceptively fast clown was putting even more miles between us and the circus: I was being carried away at a lightning pace.

And then, all at once, Cheapteeth stopped running and cast my head away like an old potato as he dropped onto his knees.

"Just you and me now, Ed," he growled, his peeling makeup plastered to his sick, lopsided face with a mixture of spittle and blood. "Just you and me."

"I beg to differ."

Looking back, I think I saw the outline of Evil Clive even before Cheapteeth managed to stagger back onto his feet.

"You think you can save him?" the clown gabbled, waddling over to my disembodied head and resting one of his big slippers on my cheek. I felt like a football at kickoff.

It was *so* humiliating. My hatred for Cheapteeth was practically electric. I could feel a surging wave of angry power shifting through my soul. It felt like a pulse had suddenly begun to beat in my temple, but only the gods knew what was causing such a swelling—not blood, that was certain!

Evil Clive took a step to one side and tipped his skull at an odd angle, almost as if he was listening for something. "Your souls will perish together," he said, at length. "You and the thing that took possession of his arm in your sick bargain with the devil."

I felt confused. Surely it was Cheapteeth himself who'd taken possession of my arm when I'd first died?

"You don't know what you're dealing with." The clown laughed. He lifted his foot from my head, then took a quick run up and kicked it aside, passing it across the open ground as Clive advanced on him. "That arm now has the devil's fingers . . . and those extra digits now do *his* work. . . ."

"Not if Ed can control it."

"Ha! A child's mind against the will of the devil himself? Don't make me laugh."

The world spun around and around as my head rolled over and over on the dirt. If it wasn't for my nose, I figure I'd have rolled quite smoothly. As it was, I felt like I'd been punched in the face about forty-seven times. The final roll ended with a sickening crack that I just knew was the bridge of my nose actually breaking. I was barely aware of Evil Clive slamming into Kambo Cheapteeth like a rogue missile . . .

. . . and, then, as the two undead warriors rained terrible blows on each other, I began to feel it advancing toward me . . .

. . . my arm . . .

. . . the devil's arm!

TWELFTH MISTAKE:

LOSING CONTROL

When something terrible happens, you always look back and feel that there's more you could have done. This is a normal, healthy reaction to horrible events, but, sadly, you're often wrong. On some occasions, it doesn't matter what you try to do: it's like the films you watch where the guy keeps going back in a time machine and doing things over but can't seem to sort out *any* of the stuff he's trying to fix.

As the ferocious, electric battle between Evil Clive and Kambo Cheapteeth unfolded in Midden Field, I quickly realized that there was simply nothing I could do to help.

There were grades of the dead, you see. Clive had been dead longer than anyone else in Mortlake and had, I assumed, become privy to certain grave-risen abilities, and Kambo Cheapteeth had evidently learned many of the same skills while drawing weird circles in the back of his carnival caravan. Watching the two of them duke it out was like watching Yoda take on the Emperor.

So, being a head lying in a field with no visible means of movement and only a single good pupil to observe anything with, I took the one course of action available to me.

I closed my eyes and stretched out with my feelings.

There was my torso: I could feel it being held by someone, maybe even carried along. The wind on my chest felt as fresh and icy as it would have had the torso still been attached to me.

Odd.

My legs felt the same way; a rush of wind

and the physical support of arms wrapped around them. Also, I could feel my foot, as if it had been reattached.

What *was* going on? I needed to get back to the circus, but how?

THEN I felt it: the searing, magnetic power of the hand. I'd barely *thought* of it when I suddenly had a vision of grasslands passing by at high speed. It was approaching Midden Field.

There was no more time.

It was here.

The arm sprang into the air, and I noticed it was now covered in the same sickly black liquid I'd seen it doused in once before: a liquid that almost seemed to seep from the flesh.

The devil's blood?

As I watched with mounting horror, it fastened onto the bony neck of Evil Clive. The zombie faltered slightly, releasing his grip on

Cheapteeth long enough for the clown to roll aside and stagger away.

Shadows were beginning to approach on all sides of the clearing—familiar shadows.

Two werewolves were supporting Max Moon, who appeared to be barely conscious. Forgoth the Cursed had regained control of Mumps: the free-roaming demonic entity was now languishing in its disguise as a small, stuffed teddy bear. Behind them, two young vampires I didn't know were carrying both halves of my body. This totally freaked me out—especially when the taller one patted my leg as if it was an elderly dog he was carrying.

They all stopped, hanging on the edge of the clearing as if they'd hit some sort of invisible force field. They looked petrified by what they saw.

The arm had full control of Evil Clive: a grim, watery blue outline had settled around the leader of Mortlake's undead community... and he was becoming slightly blurred.

Cheapteeth stood on the far side of the clearing. The clown was still laughing maniacally, but his features were twisted in a kind of fascinated horror at the situation unfolding before him.

"Ed," Clive called weakly, turning his empty eye sockets toward the patch of grass where my head still rested. "H-help me."

"How?" I cried, feeling confused and pathetically useless in the gathering darkness.

"T-take controoolllllllll."

I focused all my energy and attention on my body, feeling my mind bleed into a sharp point as the pain of my own death resurfaced. I saw the truck, felt the despair, felt the . . .

. . . anger.

My torso flew from the grip of the smaller vampire and hit the field, sliding across the grass and connecting with my head. There was a slow sort of sucking noise as the bones fused together. I thought I might throw up, but I was quickly distracted when my legs followed suit, slipping underneath the midsection and propelling me onto my feet.

Both feet.

I looked down at the toes that had deserted me on the high wire and noticed that one of them twitched, slightly.

There was only one more thing missing.

I made a straight dash for Evil Clive and my other arm but was intercepted midway by Kambo Cheapteeth, who barreled into me with far greater strength than I'd previously given him credit for.

We both went flying.

All around the clearing, my friends stood by, frozen to the spot with fear as Clive struggled to free himself from the death grip of the devil's fingers.

I couldn't even begin to help.

I was in the fight of my undead life.

Kambo Cheapteeth wasn't messing around. His desire to kill me was now so powerful that the demented clown was like a wild animal, kicking, biting, and clawing at me with spit flying from his lips in all directions.

Astonishingly, I felt calm.

My mind was elsewhere.

As Cheapteeth dragged me down to the ground and hammered a flurry of punches into my fleshless skull, I concentrated all my mental energy into releasing my detached hand's grip from the neck of Evil Clive. After all, four of the nine fingers on that hand might belong to the devil . . . but the rest were *mine.*

And then, half dazed by the insanely pow-erful punches of Kambo Cheapteeth and half tortured by the effort of telepathy required to control my arm, I finally managed to break the deadlock.

Evil Clive dropped to the floor . . . and my arm shot back across the clearing.

Kambo Cheapteeth's expression went from sheer glee at the damage he was doing to a shocked, bulging-eyed, distinctly throttled gri-mace as the demon hand fastened on his neck.

NOW, I thought. *Now we'll see. I've been in this very field—in this fight—before . . . and last time I won.*

The arm socket reattached to my shoulder with the same wet, sucking noise, and I pow-ered to my feet, feeling a fresh burst of energy as Cheapteeth visibly weakened in the grip of the demon hand.

I tightened my grasp on the clown, forcing him onto his knees. Cheering erupted from all around the clearing.

I grinned over at Max, who smiled back at me with vague comprehension as Kambo withered even further, shrinking up as he made a last ditch attempt to fight me off.

But his struggles were futile.

Still, my death grip tightened on his painted neck…and now I saw a look of panic flood through the clown's twisted face.

Did I need to destroy him?

Of course I did.

I grinned maniacally. New power coursed through my dead veins. I remembered every punch the clown had given me, every strike against my flesh.

I tightened my grip and watched the life seep out of the wretch's sallow face.

Then, all at once, Evil Clive appeared on the edge of my vision, creeping closer until he stood on the other side of the clown now wriggling weakly in my demonic grasp.

"Don't do it, Ed."

I glanced up at him. "What? Are you crazy? He would have destroyed me! He cursed me to live out this whole horrible nightmare! Don't you get it? He's never going to leave me alone! Not unless I finish it *now....*"

The skeleton shook his head.

"There are other ways. Besides, it's not you doing the thinking. Let go of him. Let go of him NOW."

I tried to listen, but Clive's voice was like a tiny trickle of water in the rushing rapids of my anger.

Powerless to stop myself, I squeezed until my soul screamed out in rage, until my teeth ground together with a sickening crunch.

Clive looked down at my arm and took hold of it with both his skeletal hands. But I continued to close the vise on Cheapteeth.

A gasp went up from the audience in the clearing.

Then it happened.

My clawed, nine-fingered hand crushed the light from Kambo Cheapteeth. The clown's dirty, mud- and paint-encrusted face sagged suddenly, and a glowing blue light drifted from between his lips and floated upward.

I watched, my stomach turning over as the light floated into the sky . . .

. . . and then everything was a blur.

I awoke from my momentary dazzle still in the field and still surrounded by my undead friends . . .

... but none of them were smiling. Two of the vampires were holding back the were-wolves, while little Forgoth was shaking with terror.

I couldn't understand what was happening or how much time had passed in my impromptu daydream.

Then everything became clear, as if someone had suddenly switched on all my senses.

And there was Max Moon.

The werewolf had managed to stagger across the clearing and was wrenching at my demon hand with all his might, screaming at me to take control of myself.

"Ed! ED! Can you hear me? ED! It's me, Max. ED!"

My voice growled forth in a dark and menacing tone that even I didn't recognize.

"NO, MAX. I WILL NOT STOP."

"Ed! You have to stop now! Look what you're doing! LOOK!"

I shook my head as violently as I could to try to break free of the miasma surrounding me. When I did, and finally managed to look down, I gasped out loud.

I was killing Evil Clive.

My choking grip had transferred from the deflated clown to the skeleton, and now I couldn't stop my own onslaught. I was killing the beloved leader of Mortlake's undead community … and my savagely wounded best friend was trying desperately to drag me away.

As I fought to stop my addled mind from fizzing up, I tried to drive my thoughts to happier times: to my parents, to my life before the accident. I tried to think of every single thing that had ever made me happy and all the things that might *still* make me happy if I managed not to do this terrible, terrible thing.

I thought of Jemini sitting up in bed, released from the curse of Kambo Cheapteeth and his horrible midget conjurer; I thought of Max and me laughing at the weirdness of Mrs. Looker's collapsing house.

I thought of being in a *happy place* in Mortlake, condemned to live out the rest of my undeath as a skeletal zombie, but surrounded by friends who never left my side …

… condemned … to live … as a zombie.

Cursed.

Locked forever in the land of the dead.

I cast a last, terrified, pleading glance at Max Moon, and then I saw the horror in my best friend's face...

...as I completely destroyed Evil Clive.

REASON . . . TO AVOID CHEESE:

It's mad, bad, and dangerous to chase

The test finally happened at what I guessed was about mid-afternoon the following day.

The bolts on the great door slid back as usual, but then there was silence.

Complete silence.

Like someone who has just entered a room to find everyone staring at them with weird smirks on their faces, I moved very cautiously, expecting some horrible event to occur at any moment.

This is the test, I thought. *Expect brutality.*

I put an ear to the door (which turned out to be a mistake when I pulled away and the ear actually stayed stuck on the metal). There was an incredible lack of noise from the corridor beyond.

Nothing.

Slowly, carefully, I grasped the single iron handle on the great portal—and pulled.

Crreeeeeaaaaak.

The door swung toward me as I took several steps back—and there it was: a cold, empty passage filled with dark, gloomy shadows and only the distant flicker of torchlight.

The walls were slimy and covered in moss, the ceiling was crawling with weird insects (including something that looked like three eyeballs joined to a toe) and the floor was . . .

I looked down at the floor and did a double take.

Then I shook my head.

I even blinked to make sure I wasn't imagining things.

Nope.

There on the floor of the passage was a thick wedge of cheese attached to some sort of metal wire.

"Is this a joke?" I called out, nudging the cheese with my shoe. It moved a bit, but not much. "What's the test? To see if I try to eat it?"

There was no reply and I looked down again.

The wire pulled tight and the cheese shifted about four inches.

I didn't quite know what to do, so I called out again.

"This is ridiculous! What can this possibly pro—"

My hand twitched—not much, but slightly.

The cheese shifted suddenly—about fifty inches this time.

My hand sprang out, clawed at the mossy wall, and dragged me forward. I used my other hand to slow my progress, but when I looked back the cheese was once again on the move.

"What the heck is—"

I punched myself in the face. It wasn't that hard, but I wasn't expecting it. The blow smashed my crumbling nose and almost knocked me over.

Screaming in anger, I rallied back and gave my left arm such a slap that even the elbow flushed red.

Then the cheese went nuts. It must have been pulled so hard on the wire that it actually took off into the air, flying away from me like a weird, cheddar version of Superman. My evil appendage backhanded me for good measure and then dug into the moss, dragging me along like a little kid pulls a new kite. I was ramming into walls, tripping over rocks, colliding with unseen trees growing from the path.

And, all the while, I'm thinking: *This is mental.*

The cheese shot up the spiralling steps of the Well, and I went after it. I couldn't help picturing a massive mousetrap waiting at the end of the wire to signal a hefty goodbye to what was left of my crumbling body.

"Argghh!" I screamed as my head glanced off yet another rock, and then I was out—emerging from the top of the well into the dank, glistening tunnels of the sub-sewer.

I couldn't even see the cheese anymore; it was a distant memory.

Then it happened.

Crossing from the sub-sewer into one of the old underground tunnels, my demonic arm swung me around the bend with such force that my head smacked sharply off an ancient brick outcrop and I was immediately knocked unconscious.

I had one very quick and unusual dream where I was riding an elephant with chronic diarrhea through a garden of enormous vegetables. Then I woke up . . .

. . . and soon wished I hadn't.

My head was still bouncing off something, and I was still being propelled along. But now I felt a cool carpet of grass passing underneath me. Somehow, my loss of consciousness had seen me through three different sets of underground tunnels and now I was back above ground, heading for—what?

I managed to glance up just in time to see

the grim outline of Mortlake Church against the background of a dark night sky.

I could now see the cheese flying toward it, the wire dragging it so fast that it actually sprang up in places, ricocheting off rocks and losing parts of its mass in bushes and hedgerows along the way.

It wasn't even cheese shaped any more. It closely resembled a slightly weather-beaten block of butter.

I risked another glimpse forward, thinking at first that the entrance to the church was actually wreathed in flame. In fact, the flames were from torches carried by a large group of cloaked and hooded figures that gathered in a rough semicircle on the church steps. A little way behind them, and slightly off to one side, stood Max Moon and Jemini, both looking as worried as I felt.

Flames, said my ever-annoying subconscious. *They're going to burn you.*

But—seriously—what could I do? I quickly assessed my options. I came up with:

- Dig my good hand into the grass and get it ripped off.
- Dig my good hand and my legs into the grass and get them all ripped off.
- Dig my good hand and my legs into the grass, stop my progress, have a massive fight with my other hand—lose—and get ripped apart.
- Dig my good hand and my legs into the grass, stop my progress, have a massive fight with my other hand—win—and get burned alive by the town torch bearers.
- Wait and see what happens.

Guess which one I went for?

Trying to block out the weird chanting that I could now hear ringing clearly from the fast-approaching church entrance, I drew in a breath, thought of my friends, and prepared to take one for the team.

I could never have predicted what happened next. . . .